W9-BHG-814

This book belongs to

Caileigh

Dora's READY-TO-READ Adventures

Based on the TV series *Dora the Explorer*® as seen on Nick Jr.®

No part of this publication may be reproduced, stored in a retrieval system,
or transmitted in any form or by any means, electronic, mechanical, photocopying, recording,
or otherwise, without written permission of the publisher. For information regarding permission,
write to Simon Spotlight, Simon & Schuster Children's Publishing Division,
1230 Avenue of the Americas, New York, NY 10020.

ISBN 0-439-72388-4

Dora's Picnic; Follow Those Feet!; and *Dora in the Deep Sea* copyright © 2003 by Viacom International Inc.
I Love My Papi! and *Say "Cheese!"* copyright © 2004 by Viacom International Inc.
NICKELODEON, NICK JR., *Dora the Explorer,* and all related titles, logos, and characters
are registered trademarks of Viacom International Inc. All rights reserved.
Published by Scholastic Inc., 557 Broadway, New York, NY 10012,
by arrangement with Simon Spotlight, Simon & Schuster Children's Publishing Division.
SCHOLASTIC and associated logos are trademarks and/or registered trademarks of Scholastic Inc.

12 11 10 9 8 7 6 5 4 3 2 1   5 6 7 8 9 10/0

Printed in the U.S.A.   23

First Scholastic printing, March 2005

These titles were previously published individually by Simon Spotlight.

Dora's READY-TO-READ Adventures

SCHOLASTIC INC.

New York   Toronto   London   Auckland   Sydney
Mexico City   New Delhi   Hong Kong   Buenos Aires

Contents

Dora's Picnic

8

by Christine Ricci   illustrated by Susan Hall

Hi! I am . We are
going to a picnic at Play
Park! Play Park has a ,
SLIDE
a , and .
SANDBOX   SWINGS

My **mami** is helping me make  PEANUT-BUTTER -and- JELLY sandwiches for the picnic.

 is my best friend.
BOOTS

He loves 🍌!
BANANAS

 BOOTS **has a bunch of** 🍌 **BANANAS**
for the picnic.

is riding his to
the picnic.

BENNY

BICYCLE

He is carrying juice
APPLE

in his .
BASKET

Here comes the .

BIG RED CHICKEN

The has a big of

BIG RED CHICKEN BAG

for the picnic.

POPCORN

Yummy!

Look!  **BABY BLUE BIRD** has a bowl of fruit in her  **WAGON**.

The fruit bowl has ,
, and .

BANANAS

APPLES

GRAPES

What did  bring to the picnic?

TICO

 brought .

TICO   BREAD

The is filled with

          BREAD

 and !

BLUEBERRIES   NUTS

ISA made **CUPCAKES** to share with everyone.

I like chocolate  CUPCAKES
with ⬤ icing. What kind
PINK
do you like?

Look out for  SWIPER.
He will try to swipe
the food we brought.

 is hiding behind

the .

Say, "Swiper, no swiping!"

Yay! You stopped !

We made it to Play Park! This  is perfect for our picnic. But first we want to play!

TABLE

likes to go down

TICO

the 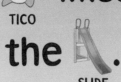.

SLIDE

27

is making a

BABY BLUE BIRD **SAND CASTLE**

in the .

SANDBOX

28

The pushes

BIG RED CHICKEN   **BOOTS**

and on the .

ISA   **SWINGS**

This is the best picnic!
We can all share the food.
What would **you** bring
to a picnic?

Follow Those Feet!

by Christine Ricci   illustrated by Susan Hall

Hi! I am **DORA**. **BOOTS** and I found some **FOOTPRINTS** in the **SANDBOX**. I wonder who made them.

Do you know?

Did I make these ?

FOOTPRINTS

No, my feet are small.

I did not make these .

FOOTPRINTS

35

Did  make these ?

BOOTS   **FOOTPRINTS**

No, his are shaped

FOOTPRINTS

like an oval. He did not

make these .

FOOTPRINTS

Who made these  ?

FOOTPRINTS

We can follow them to find out.

Hello,  !
BIG RED CHICKEN

Did you make these ?
FOOTPRINTS

No, his feet have three toes! He did not make these .

FOOTPRINTS

Did the  make
HORSE
these ?
FOOTPRINTS

40

No, the horse wears  **HORSESHOES**
on her feet. She did not
make these 🐾. **FOOTPRINTS**

41

Did the  CROCODILE make these footprints?

No, the  has long

CROCODILE

nails. He did not make

these  .

FOOTPRINTS

43

Did the  make the _?
RABBIT   FOOTPRINTS

No, she has two long feet

and two short feet.

She did not make these

 FOOTPRINTS

Did the  make these  ? No, the  does not have feet!

SNAKE

FOOTPRINTS

SNAKE

He slides across the
ground. He did not make
these .

FOOTPRINTS

Do you see ? Did
SWIPER   SWIPER

make these ?
FOOTPRINTS

No,  is sneaky!
SWIPER
He tiptoes. He did not
make these .
FOOTPRINTS

The  go all the way to
FOOTPRINTS
the beach!

They go by the  SHELLS

toward the .
SAND CASTLE

Now do you know who
made these ?
FOOTPRINTS

It was  ! He walked to
BENNY

the beach in his new  !
FLIPPERS

Yay! We did it! We found
out who made the !
FOOTPRINTS

Dora in the Deep Sea

NICK JR. DORA the EXPLORER

by Christine Ricci   illustrated by Robert Roper

Hi! I am .
DORA
This is .
BOOTS

And here is our friend,

. looks sad.
PIRATE PIG **PIRATE PIG**

What is wrong, ?
PIRATE PIG

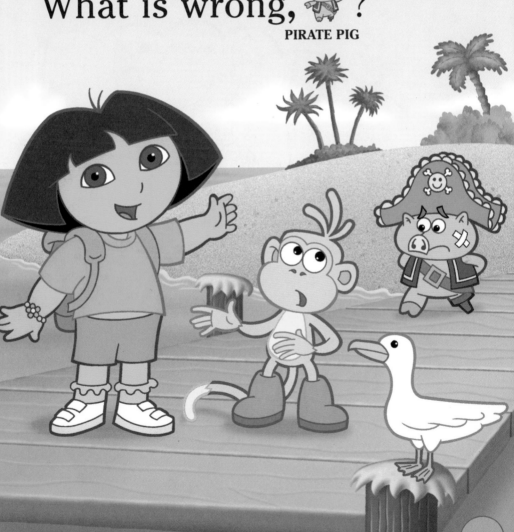

"I have lost my !"

TREASURE CHEST

says  . "The

PIRATE PIG   **TREASURE CHEST**

fell off my and

SHIP

into the !"

SEA

58

BOOTS and I will help **PIRATE PIG**

find his  .
TREASURE CHEST

Will you help too?

We need something to take us down into the  .
SEA
What can take us into the
SEA ?

A can take us down

SUBMARINE

into the  !

SEA

Ooh, we are going down into the  .

SEA

Look! A  !

SAND CASTLE

Hello,  !

KING CRAB

There is a  FISH with SPOTS

by the ROCK .

64

I see a  . . . and a funny

STARFISH

clownfish!

Boots spots a  GREEN TURTLE .

Pirate Pig sees YELLOW SEA HORSES .

66

Oh, no! Here come some

 !

LOBSTERS

They will try to pinch

the  with their 🦞 !

SUBMARINE   **CLAWS**

68

We drove the 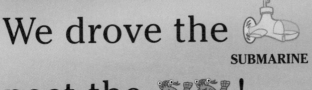 SUBMARINE

past the 🦞🦞 ! LOBSTERS

Now we need to find

the 🧰 . TREASURE CHEST

Hooray! We found

the  !

TREASURE CHEST

72

But we have to watch out

for .

SWIPER

He will try to swipe

the 📦.

TREASURE CHEST

73

Do you see 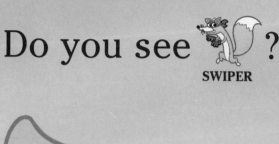?

Look! 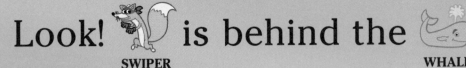 is behind the !

SWIPER

WHALE

He is going to swipe

the !

TREASURE CHEST

We have to say " , no swiping!"

SWIPER

You helped us stop !

Yay! 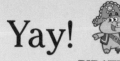 has his !

PIRATE PIG   **TREASURE CHEST**

Thank you for helping!

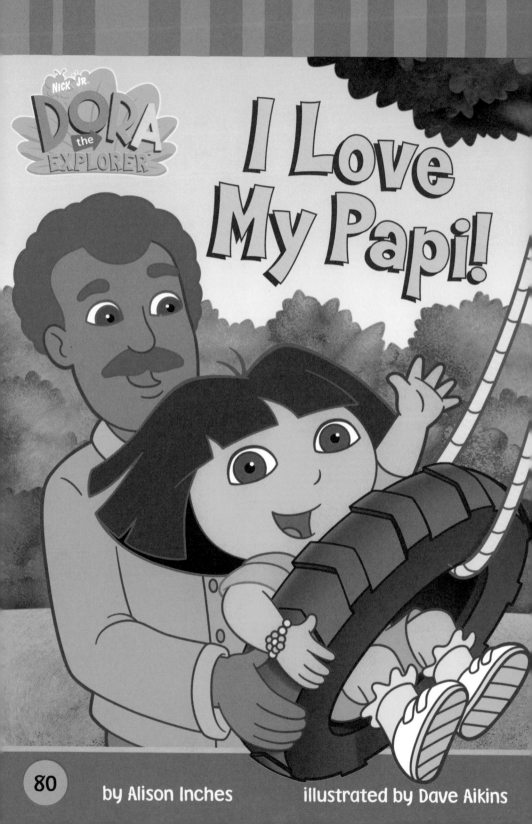

NICK JR

DORA the EXPLORER

I Love My Papi!

by Alison Inches   illustrated by Dave Aikins

My  PAPI and I love to do things together!

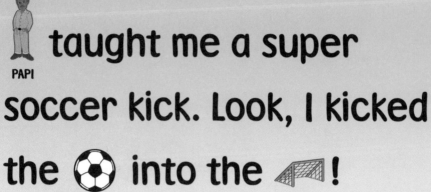 **PAPI** **taught me a super soccer kick. Look, I kicked the**  **SOCCER BALL into the** 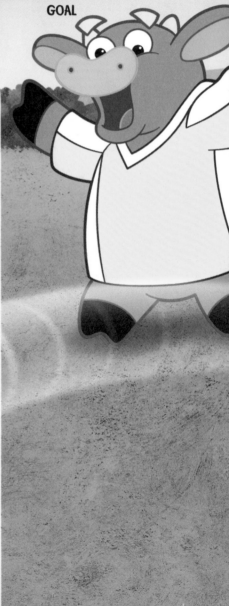 **GOAL !**

We also love playing  .

BASEBALL

PAPI coaches my team.

84

He taught us how to swing the  and slide into home .

BAT

BASE

On weekends  and I ride together.

PAPI

BIKES

Or sail on a  .

BOAT

Sometimes we go to the 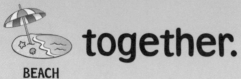 together.

BEACH

We build giant and
SAND CASTLES

play in the .
WAVES

My  is a really good .

PAPI   COOK

He taught me how to bake

a special  and make

CAKE

yummy .

SANDWICHES

90

Sometimes we pack a  PICNIC

and share it with my

friend BOOTS.

My  made us this TIRE swing! He can build anything with TOOLS.

PAPI

TIRE

TOOLS

94

One time  took us to
PAPI
the ⛺ .  loved the 🤡🤡.
CIRCUS   BOOTS   CLOWNS

96

Then  bought us  and

PAPI · POPCORN

STRAWBERRY · ICE CREAM · for a treat.

Yum! Yum!

At the end of every day  tucks me into .

PAPI

BED

Then we read a .
BOOK
I like BOOKS about ANIMALS.

101

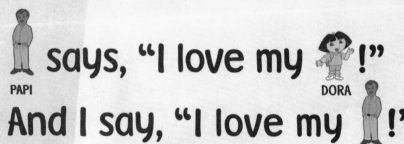 says, "I love my !"

And I say, "I love my !"

Say "Cheese!"

by Christine Ricci   illustrated by Steven Savitsky

Hi! I am . My friend

DORA   BOOTS

is sick today.

How can we cheer him up?

I know! We can visit

BOOTS

at his .

TREE HOUSE

And we can use my

CAMERA

to take pictures of things

 likes.

BOOTS

BOOTS would love a picture

of and .

BACKPACK **MAP**

Say " !"

CHEESE

107

We are at Mountain.
STAR
 Mountain is filled
STAR
with .
STARS
 loves to play with
BOOTS
the !
STARS

Look! There is .

TOOL STAR

 has all kinds of .

TOOL STAR TOOLS

Say " !"

CHEESE

Here is a fruit garden.

Which fruit does  like?

Yes,  loves !

BOOTS

BOOTS

BANANAS

Who else loves ?
BANANAS

The 🐦!
BIRD

Say "🧀!"
CHEESE

likes silly things too!

BOOTS

The  are making silly

CROCODILES

faces.

112

Ha, ha, ha! Smile,  !

CROCODILES

Say "  !"

CHEESE

Do you see more

silly things?

has baked a

ISA CAKE

for .

BOOTS

Yummy!

114

made a  for .

BENNY   CARD   BOOTS

 and look at

ISA   BENNY

the .

CAMERA

Say "  !"

CHEESE

likes to swing
BOOTS

through the .
JUNGLE

 likes to swing
DIEGO

through the too!
JUNGLE

 likes to play

BABY JAGUAR

in the .

FLOWERS

Say "  !"

CHEESE

Here is an cart.

ICE-CREAM

 loves !

BOOTS   ICE CREAM

Say " !"

CHEESE

Uh-oh. Do you see someone behind the cart?

ICE-CREAM

It is !
SWIPER

 wants to swipe
SWIPER

our .
CAMERA

We have to stop .

SWIPER

Say " , no swiping!"

SWIPER

121

Yay! We stopped !

Hey, there is !

SWIPER

TICO

 will give us a ride

TICO

to the  in his .

TREE HOUSE   CAR

Say " !"

CHEESE

123

Hooray! We made it to the

TREE HOUSE .

And loves all the

BOOTS

pictures!

We cheered up  .
BOOTS
Thanks for helping!

Oh, I have to take 1
ONE

more picture.

 wants a picture of

BOOTS

you!

Say " ![] !"

CHEESE